UNTO

A MODERN REIMAGINING OF DANTE'S PARADISO

HEAVEN

SAMUEL FLEMING

Cover art by MiblArt

ISBN-13: 978-1-954679-37-5 (paperback)
ISBN-13: 978-1-954679-36-8 (ebook)

Thank you to my Beta Readers

and to my First Reader,

Mel.

iv

Contents

The Top of the Mountain of Purgatory

What does it feel like to stand on the brink?

The mountain of Purgatory sits atop a lone island in an endless expanse of ocean. Spirits of the deceased mull about the walls, awaiting the privilege to enter Ostia. The city wraps around the mountain, seven Terraces spiraling around its sheer face. It's a city removed from time, adorned with a mosaic of cultures and people that *believed*, yet must cleanse their souls before their ascent to Heaven.

Each Terrace marks a test of the soul, one that can only be passed by extolling one of the Seven Virtues—the opposite of their Hellish counterparts. Though Purgatory holds none of the horrors of Hell, it holds turmoil and pain of a different kind. One must come to terms with their sins and failings in life.

It can take years to embody just one virtue and lifetimes to climb the entire mountain.

Lieutenant Hector Ramirez climbed the mountain in two days.

Guided by Virgil Maro and driven by forces he does not understand, he has made it through Hell, and now Purgatory. The pain of Hell was replaced with the struggle and healing of the mountain.

Ramirez was standing in a small clearing in the forest atop the mountain of Purgatory. The salt smell and crashing of ocean waves that had been so persistent in his climb were replaced with the smell of pine and earth, and silence. His muscles burned dully from the two-day climb and from the challenges.

Virgil, his ever-present guide through both Hell and Purgatory, left him at the top of the mountain. As an unbeliever, Virgil wasn't permitted to go further. And at the top of the mountain, Hector found his grandfather Gaspar, Hector's rock through much of his young life and now his guide through Heaven.

What does it feel like to stand on the brink?

To Lieutenant Hector Ramirez, it felt like warm sun on his face.

Hector said, "I don't think I'm ready." The two men still hadn't moved from their spot in the clearing.

Lito Gaspar set a hand on his grandson's shoulder. "No one ever thinks they are. That's what faith is for. Trust in something higher than yourself, and you will see the truth."

"What is that?" Hector asked.

"That you have always been ready. You just needed a little guidance, *and to make a choice.*"

The soldier smiled warmly and shook his head, not at the statement, but at his Lito Gaspar, who looked like he stepped out of Hector's childhood memory. Deep set wrinkles across his face and his flannel shirt, the sleeves always rolled up.

The same voice that had cheered and consoled the young boy.

There was half a lifetime of things Hector wanted to say to his abuelo. Things he wanted to tell Gaspar about.

"Words aren't enough," Hector finally said. He doubted they ever would be.

Gaspar smiled. "Many times they aren't, but we have time. Maybe when we get there, the words will come to you easier."

Gaspar turned and led Hector a few steps over to the center of the clearing. The sky above was bright blue with thin, wispy clouds. The sun was somewhere beyond the treeline. Soon the sky would bleed with sunset.

But they would not be there.

"What happens now?" Ramirez asked, half-joking. "I came here on a C-130. Are they bringing us a Blackhawk?"

Gaspar smirked. "Oh, no. This trip is *a little* different." Then he looked upward. "A little like flying. Come, stand beside me, and look up at the sky."

Ramirez had been about to ask: A little like flying, but in *what,* exactly? But as the soldier stepped next to his abuelo and looked up at the sky, childlike wonder overcame him, and Hector knew what Gaspar meant.

The ground left his feet, and Ramirez's stomach lurched at sudden weightlessness. Hector looked to his grandfather and saw the treeline of the forest receding from view. The next moment, the forest and the top of the mountain was gone, and the wind roared around them.

"Look up!" Gaspar shouted.

Hector turned to the sky, eyes squinted against the rushing wind, just in time to see the white of the clouds and the blue of the sky disappear. The torrent of wind was replaced with silence, the cool air with nothingness.

The stars were so bright that they glittered like diamonds.

"Is—Are we?" Ramirez turned to his grandfather and saw a smile on the old man's face.

"Yes, we're flying through space. We've got a minute or two before we get to the moon if there's anything you want to talk about."

~ ~ ~

First Sphere: The Moon and the Inconsistent

"Wait, we're going to the moon?"

"First stop." Gaspar replied.

Ramirez turned from the eerie star speckled emptiness to regard his abuelo. His gray hair and shirt collar were fluttering in wind that wasn't there; Hector's fatigues were doing the same.

"What's that about?" Hector asked tentatively. "There's no wind in space."

Gaspar glanced at his collar and up to his hair and then chuckled. "I guess you're going to see a lot of that on this journey." When Gaspar saw his grandson's face, he continued, "A lot of things that don't make sense: Cities on the moon and on other planets. Just remember that we're not in the world of the living right now and that the planets don't abide by the same rules as they would if we were alive—don't get hung up on the details, Nieto."

Ahead, the moon hung small against the black. For a moment, Ramirez had lost all sense of movement—he no longer felt wind against his skin and the stars were so far away they didn't seem to move at all. Then the moon began to grow. In moments, Ramirez could see impact craters...

And then he saw lines on the surface—not just lines, but structures.

The surface of the moon grew so wide that it filled his vision. Sprawling cities dotted the surface, their roads and buildings arranged in interlocking geometric shapes. All the cities and structures were the same gray as the moon expanse between them.

They quickly descended toward one city in particular, past the tops of massive, blocky skyscrapers, and Hector marveled at how the city seemed to sprawl upward as well as outward. So close then, that it seemed that instead of just being the same color as the moon dust, the buildings were *exactly* the same color—as if they were made from the dust.

People stared out through window cutaways in the gray stone and mulled about on the streets.

As Ramirez and Gaspar descended below the buildings, their speed slowed considerably until they were merely falling instead of soaring. Then still slower, until they were floating down the few stories feet first.

Gaspar was aiming for a small clearing between the buildings. For a small patch of green amongst the gray.

It wasn't until they were nearly landed that Hector realized that the familiar sensations of earth—or land—had returned. He felt the breeze again, and heard the bustling crowds and conversations on the streets below.

The two landed in a small park, and the crowd parted only slightly to accommodate their arrival. Ramirez's feet touched the ground and he breathed a sigh of relief. As wondrous as the sensation of flight had been, it was something completely alien and he was thankful to be standing still again—even if it was on the moon.

Hector nudged at the grass and the gray dirt with his boot, before taking in the sight. The park covered what might have been two or three old city blocks. Most of this was occupied by people who mulled around conversing. There were no statues or monuments, and Hector saw only a few shrubs and bushes scattered about.

The people struck him equally. They were a beautiful mix of races and statures, just as he had seen on the Terraces of Ostia in Purgatory, but all the people here wore the same muted gray robes. A few might've worn shades of blue, but that was it. Ramirez looked up, following the gray stone buildings and the staggering heights of muted skyscrapers.

Ramirez shook his head in disbelief. How could Heaven be both a marvel and be so sullen? The only color came from the people and the grass. Even the conversations around him reminded him of Purgatory. God—even Purgatory had color, art, and music. Even Limbo had that!

Hector stammered, "Something must be wrong here."

"What is it, Nieto?" Gaspar asked.

Ramirez explained the lack that he felt and the muted eeriness of the place.

Gaspar sighed. "I warned you that the spheres of Heaven would not abide by the same rules."

"I can understand breathing on the surface of the moon or flying through space, but this is Heaven, Lito! Shouldn't

Heaven be warm and beautiful? It's supposed to be a refuge…"

"There *is* beauty here, Hector," his grandfather said patiently. "It is just not the same as you expected. You're not dead, neither are you a believer, and so you do not feel the light of the Lord as those here feel it, or as I feel it. Here, Faith provides much.

"But you are right that *something* is missing here," Gaspar added. "Each Sphere of Heaven is centered around a different virtue. The outermost three Spheres are composed of those whose virtues were deficient, and so you will feel a lack in those Spheres. The moon is the outermost Sphere, and inhabited by the faithful that were inconsistent in their faith…

"You know a thing or two about that, don't you, Nieto?"

Gaspar's voice was quiet but stern. Ramirez heard his grandfather, but as he looked at the buildings and to the people, the soldier was still dumbfounded by the sight of it all.

"There are so many here," Hector mumbled.

"Most are inconsistent," Gaspar said with a shrug. "And so most souls exist in the First three Spheres."

"What about the other Spheres?" Ramirez asked. "Do people still try to ascend to the upper levels?"

Gaspar stared at his grandson, seemingly searching for the words. "I think you misunderstand. For these souls, there is no higher place to go. They live here in the First Sphere because they lived a faithful, but inconsistent, life. But even here on the moon, they still live in Heaven, and still feel the Heavenly light just as they would as if they lived in the Sphere of the saints or of the angels—all Spheres exist within the heart of God."

"But I do not feel the light?"

"Not yet," Gaspar said, wagging a finger. "But you will. As we go from Sphere to Sphere, we will get closer and closer to God. You will find it easier to feel His light the further we go."

Ramirez looked hesitantly at the people around them and the gray stone that loomed above.

"Do you need a different explanation, Nieto?" Gaspar asked.

"No..." Ramirez met his abuelo's eyes and struggled to find the words.

Standing on the surface of the moon, in the First Sphere of Heaven itself, and Ramirez still felt doubt. It was like a nagging sore that wouldn't quite heal. One that he'd had since he was a boy—since his father left.

Ramirez could hear every platitude and cliche said to him over the years: 'The Lord works in mysterious ways', or 'He won't give you more than you can bear', or worse, that it was all 'part of His plan'. None of which comforted the young boy, much less the angsty teenager or the doubting man that Ramirez turned out to be.

Standing in the First Sphere of Heaven, Ramirez felt the furthest from God that he had ever been.

How could he possibly tell that to his abuelo, his guide?

With a specter's patience, Gaspar waited.

And all Ramirez could finally say was, "I still do not believe."

Gaspar put a hand on his grandson's shoulder. "Let's talk about it. After all, that's why I'm here."

~

Hector followed his grandfather across the park to a short wooden bench along the outskirts. The mass of people—souls—spread out before them while their backs were to one of the massive buildings.

The weary soldier leaned back against the stone. Its surface felt neither cold nor warm, merely rough behind him. He ran a hand over the wood slats of the bench, trailing a finger through the grains.

"I'm in Heaven and I don't believe," Ramirez scoffed.

"One can see a great many things and not believe their eyes." Gaspar sat beside him, arms across his chest and resting on the small hump of his belly.

"But I never did, Lito. I don't think I ever believed."

It was his grandfather's turn to scoff. "You must have, or you would not be here. Virgil and I wouldn't have brought you."

Hector thought back on his life. So much had been colored by his father's leaving. Sometimes it felt like he had lived every waking day in the shadow of a man who was barely there. That father-figure shaped hole had been filled by his abuelo, as best as it could be, and by the Lord—another absentee father figure.

"I believed because *you* did," Hector muttered. "Because Mom did. It wasn't me, it was the people around me. Even in Omega Squad, I didn't believe. I was just using the tools I had. Using my squad. Even when we were fighting demons…"

Gaspar waved a dismissive hand. "You don't have to recount or repent or ask forgiveness. Not here. I do want you to quit being so hard on yourself. Is life not hard enough as it is? Where is the fairness in being hard on yourself when you've endured so much."

"I've had it easier than most."

"Harder than others," Gaspar replied. "You were stronger than a boy your age had any right to be, and you did right by your mother. And you still chose a harder path! You joined up with the military and then with Omega Squad. I... I know some of your thoughts, Nieto—not all, but some. And I do not wish to know them all. You and your men lived through horrors that no man should have to face.

"You've grown. You might not see it, but I do. And in more than just your years. I can see why you were chosen."

Ramirez turned from the crowd to his grandfather. "Virgil once said something similar. He said there were others that had gone on this journey through Hell, Purgatory, and now here... Why me, Lito? Why me?"

HIs grandfather wagged a finger again. "Now, I've got and said too much! It is not my place to tell you why, Hector. But I promise you that before this is through, you will know why you were chosen."

Ramirez turned back to the quiet crowd and sighed in frustration. *That* was something, he supposed. He thought of Omega squad—his squad—and all the others that had been sent into that unholy cavern. So many souls traded just for him. Just for one.

Ramirez said sarcastically, "Maybe by then I'll know if it was all worth it."

The soldier turned to his grandfather, but Gaspar hung his head. Ramirez had been ready for a platitude or an explanation, and couldn't tell whether he was more grateful or distraught that his grandfather had nothing to offer him.

"I'm sorry," Ramirez said, afraid he had offended his abuelo. "Of all people, I'm not angry with you."

"I know," Gaspar said plainly. "You have every right to be angry. It's only natural. But I want you to know that some of your men made it out of Hell."

Ramirez shook his head. "I don't understand. I saw them—all of them—fall."

"That doesn't mean that they stayed there. Turner and Smith were lifted up to Purgatory. You just didn't see them at the city gates because your journey was so quick and the crowd was very big. There were a lot of folk you would've recognized... Anyway, those three are in a better place, though they have a long journey ahead of them."

Ramirez nodded, and bittersweet tears welled behind his eyes. That was better than he hoped, but there were still so many of them trapped below. More of them deserved to be saved.

Virgil had said *there were no perfect persons in Heaven; all had their shortcomings. But there were equally good persons in the Circle of Limbo, for no reason other than their birthrights.*

"Thank you for that," the Lieutenant said to his grandfather. "Thank you," he said again to whoever else might be listening.

~

The pair sat on the bench in the park a while longer.

In spite of being in Heaven and on the moon, Ramirez found himself talking about everything else.

He told his abuelo about the years that he had missed. About how Anna had grown from the toddler that Gaspar had seen last, about her playing violin, and about their trips to the aquarium. And the stories turned darker. Ramirez told Gaspar about leading his squad into Hell. How they'd been picked off one by one, as the Circles trapped them according to their sins. And how his best friend had been taken by Lucifer.

Hector even narrated the scene in the icy well at the center of the underworld. Ramirez told his grandfather how eerie and beautiful Lucifer had been—the most beautiful angel. Told him how the devil had cast Sergeant Atticus Wilson down into the ice as if there had always been a spot for him there. Even told his grandfather how the devil did not want him, how his place was outside even the outermost Circle of Hell—the valley of the undecided.

Of course, Ramirez knew now why he'd been allowed to leave. Someone had plans for him. Someone that pulled the proverbial strings.

And his Lito Gaspar listened to it all, God bless him.

But Ramirez found himself skipping details as he narrated. He glossed over the grisly deaths of his squadmates—that he did for the old man's sake—but Ramirez also left out how Ramirez had been so certain that Lucifer was going to take *him* for leading his squad to their deaths. Hector omitted how Atticus had held him at gunpoint in those final moments and that his friend had pulled the trigger—how Atticus had chosen Tracey over their friendship. And left out how Lucifer had saved Hector from the gunshot.

Then Hector told his Lito Gaspar about his marriage. About how there were so many things wrong, so many warning signs that he didn't see.

"I should've known," Ramirez said. The soldier was hunched forward, chin resting on his hands. "I should've known."

Gaspar was still beside him on the bench, looking out over the crowded park. "Have you thought about what you're going to tell her?"

Ramirez turned and eyed his mentor curiously. "Am I really going to get to go back?"

Gaspar chuckled. "What? Did you think we were going to keep you here?"

"No... I guess not. I'm not sure what I thought was going to happen."

"I imagine you're here to learn a lesson."

"And what might that be?"

Gaspar shrugged. "In Hell, you learned the truth. In Purgatory, you came to terms with it..."

"Am I here to learn how to forgive Tracey and Atticus? Or reconcile my faith?"

The old man shrugged again. "It's not my place to say."

Ramirez sighed in frustration. "That's just like you. Obtuse when you were living *and* when you're dead!"

Gaspar smiled and slapped his grandson on the shoulder. "Do you want me to tell you something cryptic like, *in time, all will be revealed*, or would that be too much?"

For as upset as he was, Ramirez grinned. He had missed his Lito Gaspar fiercely, and seeing him again had filled a wound in his soul.

Hector playfully pushed his abuelo's arm away and then stood. "Let's get on with this ridiculousness. What realm or planet are we going to next? Mars or Pluto, maybe. Except that Pluto isn't a planet anymore."

Gaspar stood and said sarcastically, "Are you really ready, Nieto? Because we can keep sitting here on the bench."

His grandfather's words made him feel like a child again. Bashfully, he responded, "No. I'm ready to go." Then stepped forward, and both of them looked to the starry black sky.

"Good," Gaspar replied, "because Mercury is next."

~ ~ ~

Second Sphere: Mercury and the Ambitious

Ramirez didn't question it. He just resolved to follow his abuelo—wherever in the universe or in Heaven that led him.

The two men were shoulder to shoulder again, leaving the surface of the moon. The gray blocky skyscrapers of the lunar surface receded from view, and again Ramirez was surrounded by eerie calm.

Again their clothes rippled as if wind was tugging at them, but Ramirez felt nothing on his face—the wind was gone, and so was the sense of movement.

Ramirez only felt a sense of movement when he looked down and saw the moon shrinking to a dot behind him.

Hector's stomach lurched, and he quickly twisted so that he was looking ahead again. "I understand now why you told me not to do that."

Gaspar chuckled. "It's a bit disconcerting, isn't it? I still don't have the heart to look down."

"Do you do this a lot?"

"Oh no," the old man said, shaking his head. "Just a few times waiting for you to climb up the mountain."

Off to the right, the sun blazed against the blackness. They were slowly turning toward it and Ramirez shielded his eyes.

"Mercury. The closest planet to the sun, right?" Ramirez asked.

Gaspar smiled. "Good job, Nieto."

The sun grew large in their vision, easily three times larger than it looked from the Earth—even more! It felt as if they were going to fly into the very heart of it, and even though Ramirez didn't feel the cold or space or heat from the sun, he very much didn't want to fly *into the sun*. Some deep-seated fear tugged at him and Ramirez cowered from the light.

"Don't worry. Don't worry," Gaspar said and pointed slightly off to the left. "That is where we're going."

As soon as his grandfather said the words, the tiny speck that was Mercury appeared and began to swell like a balloon. The surface was a similar gray to the moon they just visited, but as the surface grew large, grids appeared on the surface. And as they grew closer, the grids became castles and walls.

Moments later, Mercury filled the horizon while the sun filled the sky to the right.

~

They touched down on a small balcony of a castle tower. Ramirez breathed a sigh of relief—the soldier didn't realize that he'd been holding his breath again.

"This is Mercury," Gaspar announced, making a sweeping gesture across the vista. "First planet from the Sun and second Sphere of Heaven."

The immediate view below was that of a castle courtyard. Statues and hedges crisscrossed below. Beyond were grid-like castle walls and parapets. Castle towers dotted the horizon.

Though the weaving mass of structures on Mercury was no grander than that of the moon, Ramirez was struck by the immensity of the sight from such a vantage. But there was something else...

"It's so... uniform," Ramirez mumbled. "The buildings here are even more uniform than the ones on the moon."

"Different rules, Nieto," Gaspar reminded him.

"I know. I know." Hector felt like a boy again—not just with his grandfather standing beside him, but with the old man's repetition as well.

The soldier turned and admired the stones that made up the balcony and the tower. They were as uniform as the notches in the parapets. From here, the stone was an off-white, rather than gray.

"So, why—"

Behind them, the balcony led to a sitting room—to a throne room. Red and gold carpet lined the room. A fireplace and several chairs sat to the left. An ornate throne sat to the right, a step above the rest, carved out of a deep red wood.

Ramirez walked tentatively into the room and found animal skins and tapestries hanging from the walls. Two of the skins might've been from lionesses, but it was hard to tell. Ramirez stared at the tapestries with the same puzzlement.

"Is that writing Greek or Roman?..."

Gaspar walked over and stood beside him. "Roman. From many, many years ago."

"Why bring me here?"

"Justinian goes out for a lot of walks, so the place is usually empty. Good view too. But there's more." His abuelo turned and pointed to the throne. "Do you see those words?

The words *'Caesar eram. Justinian sum'* were carved neatly into the back of the throne.

"It says *'Caesar I was. I am Justinian.'*"

Ramirez glanced between his abuelo and the throne. "Sorry. I'm not sure I understand."

Gaspar wagged his finger. "It perfectly captures the Second Sphere. You see, Mercury is for those believers who were too ambitious. They were deficient in the virtue of Justice."

Ramirez nodded along. "So, Caesar was too ambitious... but what about the words in the back of the chair?"

"On Earth and in life, he was Caesar, and he was motivated by Earthly things. Fame, titles, power—all things that pollute the soul. But here in Heaven he is merely Justinian. There are no titles here. He is only a man. And so his throne and all the thrones on Mercury sit empty, to remind them."

"All the people here were rulers?"

"Most. Not all though."

Ramirez nodded. "How does that apply to me, Lito? What am I supposed to learn here?"

Gaspar shrugged. "I never said this was about learning anything. *But* since you keep asking, maybe reexamine your motivations. Why did you join the service? Why join Omega Squad? Why go into Hell?"

Hector turned and paced idly between the balcony and the throne. "The service seemed like the right thing to do... It gave me direction. I joined Omega Squad because I was curious. Most couldn't stomach the training, and so I stayed because *I could stomach it*. I went into Hell because I was ordered too. And I didn't know."

"Would you have refused if you knew?" Gaspar asked.

The soldier chuckled. "I wouldn't have believed them. I would've thought it was just another plane. Just another mission."

"Why continue? Why go to Purgatory? Why come here?" Gaspar was pacing a few steps behind his grandson.

Ramirez walked to the balcony and looked out over the stone walls of Mercury. "It's just another mission and I need to see it through. I need to make it home..."

Ramirez trailed off. He needed to see Tracey and Anna again—needed to see them and needed to confront his wife. He didn't know what the Hell was going to happen after that.

She could deny it. She might leave him. There were any number of things that Tracey could do, but Ramirez wouldn't know for sure until he made it home.

Hector stared off across the horizon. Was he closer to home than before? He was on Mercury... He was the farthest from home he had ever been. Was he really trying to get home or was he just delaying it?

There was still some small quiet place within him that could pretend everything was a dream—some horrible fever dream. He was really in a jungle somewhere, waiting for the medicine to kick in. Tracey and Anna were still at home. Atticus and the rest of Omega Squad were keeping him safe while he was unconscious. There was no affair; there never had been. He would get better, make it home, and everything would be exactly as it had been before.

Of course, it was bullshit. Ramirez had been trapped on demiplanes before by witch doctors and eldritch beings. Hell, he'd been trapped in his own mind before, unable to speak or move his own limbs.

Making it through Hell, then Purgatory, and now standing on Mercury—the Second Sphere of Heaven—all that was real. He couldn't deny it. When and if Ramirez made it home, nothing would ever be the same. Even if he pretended he didn't know about the affair, even if he bottled it up and never confronted Tracey, his wife would still be devastated by the loss of Atticus Wilson—her love and Hector's best friend.

Nothing would ever be the same.

Maybe that's what his abuelo was getting at. "Do I really want to make it home?"

Hector met his grandfather's eyes and found the usual look of patience and comfort.

"Do you want to make it home, Nieto?" Gaspar echoed.

Ramirez's throat was dry and his heart was pounding. The soldier clenched his hands and shook his head. "I'm terrified. It feels like standing on the edge of a cliff."

"You need to make a choice, Hector. Not only that, but you need to make it for the right reasons. You mustn't think of it as following orders.

"Following orders will only get you so far. You accomplished much in the name of duty. You fought the supernatural, and you did so thanklessly. But your blindly following orders brought you face to face with Lucifer."

"Following orders brought me here," Ramirez added.

"Then where?" Gaspar asked. "Where do you go from here?"

Hector turned to his grandfather with quiet resolve. "I'll see this through. One Sphere after the other, and I'll see the mission through. But after this, I'm going home. I need to see Tracey and Anna. I need to talk to them. I'm not really sure what'll happen after that... But I'm doing it because I want to see it through. I *need* to see it through. And then I need to get home.

"Is that a good enough answer?"

Gaspar nodded meekly. "That's good enough, for now."

~

His resolve renewed, Ramirez turned again to the throne room. In spite of the decor, the room was sparse compared to his expectations. There was no gold, no placards, no mantles. The cloth tapestries and furniture, though ornate, were only cloth and wood.

"Gaspar, you said that most here on Mercury were rulers... How is it that they are on another Sphere of Heaven? No one really gets to choose to be a ruler... So how is that fair that they get to be on a higher Sphere?"

Gaspar smirked. "First, don't presume what's fair in light of His judgment—that's the short answer. The longer answer is this: You're right that very few get to choose to be a ruler. But the world needs all different people to function. It needs doctors, police, teachers, bakers, farmers, *lawyers*... Maybe that's too far.

"You might think that the Lord has a soft spot for rulers because He is a ruler, but that's not it. It's merely because those positions are so often called tested on the Virtue of Justice. That's all. Most people are inconsistent, and so that's why the

Moon seemed so populated. Many more reside on Venus in the next Sphere."

"Why Venus?" Ramirez asked.

Gaspar looked around the throne room one last time. "It really is a nice little place here. It suits Justinian better than his Earthly throne room. Come, Hector. I think you're ready to see the next Sphere—then I'll tell you all about it. Why don't you take one last look at that throne there. It would do you well to remember those words."

Ramirez looked at the words on the throne one last time before following his abuelo back to the balcony.

Caesar eram. Justinian sum—
Caesar I was. I am Justinian.

Ramirez didn't ask further. He figured he understood what the old man was getting at.

He was Lieutenant Hector Ramirez of Omega Squad. Here he was merely Hector Ramirez. It was simple enough.

The problem was, Ramirez wasn't worried about the soldier part of his identity. He was worried about the rest of it: Husband, father… Christian.

And those things worried him much, much more.

~ ~ ~

Third Sphere:
Venus and the Lovers

Moments later, Hector Ramirez was hurtling through space, flying from Mercury to Venus alongside his grandfather. The closest planet to the sun was already gone behind them, and in front of them, the vastness of space stretched out to infinity.

There was a lot for the soldier to contemplate, but what was on his mind at that moment was the utter size and emptiness of space. Stars that were thousands—millions—of times the size of the planets were so far away that they were nothing but pinpricks in the void. Ramirez vaguely remembered learning about space in grade school, but reading about the size and scope of the solar system—nevermind the galaxy or the universe—was meaningless. Space was just too vast for him to comprehend.

In this time in the service, Ramirez had seen the night sky from nearly every continent on Earth. Some places were so remote and removed from civilization that the stars were as bright and as clear on the ground as they were now, hurtling through space.

And despite his hurtling through space, despite being thousands of miles—millions of miles—away from Earth, Ramirez didn't feel any closer to the stars. And he wasn't any closer to understanding the true vastness of the universe than the small boy reading about it in a textbook.

Maybe there were some things that humans just weren't meant to understand. It may have been a cliché statement, but that didn't make it any less true in Ramirez's eyes.

"Penny for your thoughts," Gaspar said from beside him, hair and shirt collar fluttering in the absent breeze.

"It's just too big," Ramirez said, sweeping a hand across the void. "All that."

"Yes. Yes, it is," Gaspar said with the same sense of wonder in his voice.

"Say, Lito…" Ramirez turned and squinted at his grandfather. "Are there other things out there?"

"Oh, sure. God made all sorts of things. Eventually, we'll see the Sphere of the angels. There's all kinds of crazy looking angels."

Ramirez chuckled and shook his head. "That's not what I meant. I'm talking about aliens. You know, out there," he added, gesturing to the stars again.

"Oh! Well… What do you think, Nieto?" his grandfather asked with that familiar twinkle in his eye.

Hector sighed—the old man wasn't going to come right out and tell him. Of course, that would be too easy.

Ramirez said, "Well, I've seen enough things on Earth to know that there were things on our planet that the Lord didn't make—"

"And you're sure about that?" Gaspar squinted at his grandson.

"I've seen a lot of things on Earth," the Omega soldier repeated. "I doubt that God made all the minor deities, demons, aberrations, and other anomalies that I've encountered. And Virgil mentioned that God didn't create Hell either—that it is even older than He and Heaven."

Gaspar's expression grew serious, and he looked out across the infinite void. "I was wondering how much Virgil would tell you. How much he was allowed to tell you. The short answer is that you and Virgil are both right. *The Lord did not make all things.* There are things that are older and things that arose from the natural order."

Hector swallowed dryly. "Well, that's not what I was expecting… You're going to elaborate on that, right?"

Gaspar nodded tentatively. "Yes, but it's both hard to explain and still harder to reconcile. The things that are older are left over from other universes or things that have found their way into our Universe. Like Hell or the aberrations you speak of.

"Other things arose from the natural order—like your minor deities. Take the idea of worshiping the weather. Some phenomena are so powerful that they caused people to believe in them—that they were some intelligent, compassionate deity. In turn, the belief of people is an equally powerful thing and gives more power to those things. Some of the deities you came across were likely born in a similar fashion. Could be weather or emotion or a burial ground. Power begets worship, worship begets power, in a cycle of creation."

Ramirez looked out at the void and the stars again, feeling hollow. The existential dread that he had felt in the face of the vastness of the Universe was magnified at the echo of his grandfather's words: *The Lord did not make all things.*

Ramirez looked upon the stars as both a boy and as a man, and still could not grasp the immensity of it. What hope did he have, really? Even his creator, even the Lord, did not grasp all things.

A dot appeared in the black, orange and growing—Venus.

But there was another question that ate away at the soldier even more than those that came before. One that he both didn't want to ask and needed to ask.

As the Third Sphere of Heaven grew, Hector turned to his grandfather. "Lito, why is it taught that God made everything?"

Gaspar stared off into space, head bobbing slightly, as if he was trying to find the words. "Remember Hector, that God made *most* things... and those that he didn't are either very few or so very far away that they're an afterthought.

"Even more so, they teach that God made all things because *that belief* is very powerful. An absolute creator inspires a lot of belief, and remember that belief is power. That belief in absolute power, the Alpha and the Omega, has enabled the Lord to raise the mountain of Purgatory and to make all the Spheres of Heaven—to create other places for souls to go instead of Hell or Limbo. Enough power for the Lord to lift them up out of Hell, out of that impossibly old abyss of souls... That is a power that none other can claim."

Venus was growing large in the sky, a swirling mass of orange clouds. Ramirez was staring at it—through it. Turning his grandfather's words over.

Ramirez sighed and finally said, "That's a lot to digest."

"You've got some time."

A few moments later, the second planet from the sun stretched from horizon to horizon. Hector remembered another fact from grade school, that even though Mercury was closer to the sun, Venus was hotter—the hottest and most inhospitable place in the solar system.

As they plunged into the clouds, Ramirez turned to his grandfather, chuckled awkwardly, and asked, "So, that's a long way of saying 'yes' to aliens?"

Gaspar's serious face finally cracked into a smirk.

~

The clouds of Venus were impossibly thick and swirled around the pair like water as they descended through the clouds. Ramirez couldn't recall from grade school what chemicals made up the clouds, but he knew they weren't just water vapor like the clouds on Earth.

"Should I be glad that I can't smell right now?" Ramirez asked.

At that, Gaspar let out a hearty laugh. "Yes! Of all the beauty of Venus, the clouds are better seen and not smelt."

Ramirez glanced sideways at his abuelo. Aside from the noxious clouds, Venus was also theorized to be a barren wasteland of scorched stone. But then, the moon and Mercury hadn't been what Ramirez had expected them to be. What beauty was the old man talking about?

He didn't have to wonder for long. Moments later, the swirling orange clouds gave way, and the pair were floating toward a lush green and blue world, separated by thin strips of shoreline that twisted across the surface like cursive. Tiny huts appeared along the shore, each with a short pier. Sail boats and canoes dotted the water.

Gaspar led them down to one of the beaches on the surface. Ramirez stood for a second, dumbfounded on the beach of Venus, taking in the warm breeze and the smell of salt.

"I don't know what I expected, Lito," Ramirez said, smiling, "but this is better."

Gaspar stood beside him and rested an arm around his grandson's shoulders. "I agree. It is beautiful here. It may not be one of the higher Spheres, but this one is ours."

"This is your Sphere?" Hector asked, completely missing the nuance.

Gaspar nodded, smiling. "Mine and your abuela's."

Ramirez turned back toward the shoreline, his eyes following the wooden pier. A short, dark-haired woman was walking on the planks, toward them. A woman Hector hadn't seen in too many years.

The soldier wiped his teary eyes, cleared his throat and waved with both hands like he was a boy again. Then Hector Ramirez ran across the beach to his grandmother.

Mama Lucia was just how Hector remembered her—her warm smile, frazzled salt and pepper hair. The sleeves of her checkered shirt were rolled up.

Mama Lucia and Hector wrapped their arms around each other. Her shirt even smelled like the detergent she always used in the wash. By the time Gaspar caught up to them, there wasn't a dry eye on the beach.

Ramirez looked down at his abuela. "Lito didn't tell me that you'd be here!"

Lucia smirked and pointed to Gaspar. "Well, your abuelo didn't tell me that he was going to get you until he was walking out the door."

Gaspar held up both hands. "Hey, hey, now I know how it feels. I didn't know I was meeting Hector until then either!"

~

Hector Ramirez spent the next few hours sitting on his grandparents' pier and telling his grandmother everything he'd told Gaspar back on the Moon. He told her all about his daughter Anna, how she had grown and the beautiful girl she was growing into. And he told Mama Lucia about Hell and Purgatory, just as he had told his abuelo.

But where Lito Gaspar let Ramirez talk, Mama Lucia asked so many questions. She had always been an engaged listener, but it seemed as if she was even more curious about Hell and Purgatory than Ramirez remembered her being while she was alive.

When Ramirez's story was finally done, he asked Gaspar and Lucia about Venus and the Third Sphere of Heaven. The two had pulled their chairs close together and were sitting hand in hand.

Mama Lucia looked to Gaspar and said, "Do you want to tell him about Venus, or should I?"

Gaspar chuckled and waved his other hand dismissively. "You can tell him. I've still got a bunch more Spheres to take him to after this."

Lucia turned back to her grandson. "I know what you're thinking, Hector: That this isn't what you expected, but it really is Heaven. We want for nothing. All our family and friends—well, most of them—live down the street. Anything we want to read or watch or eat… If we want to go sailing, our boat will appear at the dock."

Ramirez smiled. "That's nice, Mama Lucia, but can you tell me more about the Sphere? So far, each has been based on a Virtue. What about here?"

She replied, "This Sphere celebrates Temperance."

"*Lack* of Temperance," Gaspar mumbled.

Lucia waved a dismissive hand. "He's right, but it's all Heaven. You'll see, Hector, that not many people made it to the final Spheres. Most of us weren't perfect, nor did we embody a specific virtue. Your abuelo is just upset that we didn't make it to a higher Sphere."

Gaspar smiled quickly. "Something like that. Your abuela is right that not many live in the higher Spheres. *The humble* live here," he added, raising his eyebrows.

Ramirez smiled at them, and then asked, "But so what should you have done better? You were the most devout Christians I ever knew."

Lucia said, "We already told you about the first three Spheres having to do with an imperfect expression of a virtue. Venus is about Temperance. Your abuelo and I loved each other very much, and we loved the Lord very much, but sometimes those two things were at conflict. Is it possible to love two people, Hector? To truly love them?"

Without hesitation, Hector shook his head. "No, I don't think it's possible."

Lucia smiled. "Most people think that way. It's the same thing as trying to believe two contradictory statements at once. Take the lake in front of us. I say, 'the water is red' or 'the water is blue'. One of those is clearly correct, clearly the truth of the moment.

"Loving God and loving another is the same—almost impossible to love them both. Even to love another *as much* as God is not right, either.

"Not to say that everyone in the Seventh Sphere was a celibate, but some of them are!" Lucia laughed.

"I imagine it helps," Gaspar added, smirking.

Ramirez chuckled along with them, but it faded quickly. "That doesn't seem fair. How can someone be that consistent? Celibacy aside… What about their parents or their family?"

Gaspar and Lucia exchanged a tentative look.

Gaspar said, "It's all Heaven, Nieto. It doesn't matter what Sphere you're in. We're all with the Lord. If you *were here*, you would feel it as surely as we do. But the closer to the center we go, the more you will feel His light."

Ramirez nodded sheepishly. *If he were here*—if he were dead and not damned to Limbo for never making a decision…

"When I was in Hell, the souls in Limbo reached out to me like I was meant to be there. When I made it to Lucifer in the center of Hell, he confirmed it…" The soldier asked hesitantly, "Can I still make a choice?"

His abuela nodded feverishly and squeezed his abuelo's hand.

"Yes, Hector," Gaspar said, voice quiet. "You can still make a choice. You can always make a choice."

Ramirez's throat suddenly grew dry with realization. "Oh God. Is that what this has all been about? Hell was about learning the truth. Purgatory was about forgiving Tracey and myself. Heaven—being here—is about finding my faith?"

This time, both his grandparents nodded meekly, as if they were afraid to answer. As if they weren't supposed to call attention to the task at hand. As if the curtain had been pulled away for the first time.

Hector stood, the chair falling dully on the pier behind him. He paced to the end of it and looked out over the lake of Venus, feeling as though his legs might collapse beneath him. His stomach turned as if it might corkscrew up and out of him.

Hands on his back—his grandparents behind him with concerned looks on their faces.

"Are you alright, Hector?" Mama Lucia asked.

Ramirez shook his head. "How can I be? All my men… All those soldiers before us—just for me? Just so I could make it here?" When the answer didn't come, Hector pulled away and turned to look at them. "That can't be. Tell me I'm wrong."

Gaspar and Lucia's faces wrinkled in concern, but neither spoke. Their silence was damning, weighing on the soldier.

The moment dragged on, filled by wind and the quiet lapping of water on the shore and against the pier.

"How long has the portal to Hell been open?" Ramirez asked.

His grandparents shook their heads. Gaspar said, "We don't know, Hector."

Ramirez sighed heavily, his voice was a hoarse whisper. "There were so many, Lito. They can't all have died just for me to get here!"

Gaspar said, "We can't know His will, and sometimes He requires sacrifice. Remember Job and Abraham. Remember, not all your men wound up in Hell. Some were—"

"Lito, please. I think… I think I need a minute alone."

Both his grandparents' faces were clouded with muted protest, but they nodded and walked away. His abuela leaning her head on his abuelo's shoulder.

Ramirez turned and sat on the edge of the pier, boots dangling above the water.

Virgil said there were others that had been chosen, others that had walked the path into Hell, up the mountain, and then come to Heaven. God, why? What was the point?

The weary soldier buried his head in his hands, and quiet tears fell onto the pier.

~

When Ramirez finally stood, his eyes were so dry they burned and his chest hurt from stifling his sobs. He had no idea how much time had passed. The sun was completely hidden behind the orange clouds.

He turned and plodded across the pier to his grandparents' hut, hands stuffed in his trouser pockets.

He was no closer to peace. No closer to absolution. In that moment, Hector Ramirez was the furthest he'd ever been from God.

Gaspar and Lucia peeked out from the backdoor, and Ramirez smiled weakly.

There was a part of him that wanted to stay and visit with his abuela. Wanted to have dinner and help with the dishes like he used to. Wanted to sit between them and fall asleep on her shoulder like he did when he was a boy.

But the rest of him knew that if he didn't keep going that he would never make it. That he would never see what he was supposed to see.

"Mama Lucia, I... I think I should be going now," Hector said, his voice trailing off. "It was good to see you."

She walked to Hector and wrapped her arms around him. "It was good to see you too, Hector. We love you very much."

Hector leaned on his grandmother as if he felt the weight of his journey—the true weight of it—for the first time. Hector sniffled and wiped his nose on his sleeve. "I love you too, Mama Lucia."

Each part of Hector Ramirez's journey had felt a little harder than the last. In that moment, letting go of his grandmother was the hardest yet.

In the end, it took his grandfather's hand upon his shoulder to snap him out of it. "Come on, Nieto. It's time for us to go."

Ramirez nodded wearily and smiled at his grandmother one last time. There were a hundred more things that he wanted to say to her. He hoped that 'I love you' would suffice.

The weary soldier turned and walked to his grandfather, before they rose together from the shore of Venus and up through the orange clouds.

~ ~ ~

Fourth Sphere:
The Sun and the Wise

From Venus, Gaspar led him back toward the sun. Despite the questions swirling in his mind, Hector could not bring himself to ask them. Venus weighed heavily on him, and Ramirez worried that it marked a turning point in his journey. And not one for the better.

So Ramirez did what he had done on so many missions, so many car rides when he was both a man and a boy—he zoned out. He stared off into the blackness of space and let the stars pass him by.

His grandfather seemed to sense this, and his old man stayed quiet for the journey. The monument of this wasn't lost on Hector; his grandfather always had some quote or advice, no matter how serious or humorous the moment.

The sun blazed bright in the sky, and the soldier squinted while looking away. But it grew larger still until Ramirez had to shield his face from it.

"Do not be afraid," Gaspar said from beside him.

Hector turned, but the sun had even blotted out his grandfather. Ramirez shut his eyes, but even that did not stop the blinding light of the sun. Hector lost control of his flight, tumbling over and over like he was tangled in his parachute. His heart pounded and he gasped for air. His fingers felt numb.

Despite his abuelo's words, Hector felt fear as they plunged into the sun.

~

"It's okay, Nieto," Gaspar said, placing a hand on Hector's shoulder to steady him.

Ramirez opened his eyes in shock, still breathing fast. He was floating down to the surface of the Sun—not flipping wildly, though his stomach didn't agree. The soldier forced himself to breathe slowly, then looked down.

The Sun was no longer just a star—no longer blinding. It was a sea of molten gold, rippling as far as he could see. In the distance, solar flares erupted, sending plumes of shimmering light impossibly high into the sky.

Ramirez had seen wonders and horrors over his short life, some of which were indescribable. Even in Purgatory, he had been overcome with awe at the sight of the Mountain of Ostia. But the solar flare rose up so high... it was like God took a paintbrush and drew from the Sun to the nearest star.

"Can you see clearly now?" Gaspar asked.

Hector nodded and looked down toward the approaching surface.

But in spite of the beauty of the shimmering surface, there was nothing on the surface. No buildings. No people.

"Lito... There's nothing here."

"We are nearly there."

Moments later, they reached the surface. In spite of the molten liquid appearance, the surface of the sun felt solid as stone beneath Hector's feet. The faintest ripples expanded from his steps.

Gaspar offered his hand. "Trust me, Nieto."

Hector took his grandfather's hand, and again, he felt like a child. His hand felt small in his elder's hand.

Gaspar suddenly fell backward, catching Hector off guard and pulling the soldier down with him. Hector reached out a hand to catch himself, but instead of landing on the shimmering surface. His hand passed through—

Ramirez flinched and closed his eyes, trying to ignore the weightless pit in his stomach. Then he was upright again.

"There, there. It's over," Gaspar said.

Hector Ramirez slowly opened his eyes. The ground—the surface of the sun—was no longer the color of molten gold, but a rippling black. It looked as if he was standing on a pane of glass and looking down at the endless abyss of starry night sky.

"Oh my God…"

Hector trailed off as he looked up. Golden towers rose up from the black, made from the same liquid gold as the surface had been moments ago. They rose, twisting and intertwining in a shimmering web nearly as high—higher even—than the solar flare.

His gaze returned, settling on the tower closest to him. It rose up hundreds of feet into the air before branching at odd, impossible angles to neighboring towers like an M. C. Escher drawing brought to life. And if Ramirez squinted, he could just make out the tiny people strolling from tower to tower like ants.

Hector's eyes wandered through the tapestry, following the odd branches until he lost his way and followed another.

"Okay, Lito. This… This *looks like* Heaven."

Gaspar smiled beside him. "It's a little gaudy for me, but it's certainly impressive. Just wait 'till you see what's inside."

~

Gaspar led Hector to the nearest tower. From so close, he couldn't crane his head back far enough to see the top. The outside had lines for brick, even though it shimmered with golden light. The entryway had similar lines for trim around the frame, but no doors.

Inside, a golden staircase spiraled around the wall, rising to a point high above—reminding Hector of a lighthouse he'd once seen as a boy. But the walls, rather than lined with stone or decorations, were lined with books of all sizes, color, and trim.

But the spines of them were blank.

It wasn't until Hector walked forward in amazement, the colors shimmered and changed, and titles seemed to light on the spines and flare into existence: An Alleged Supernatural History of America's Special Forces, Oceans of the World. Call of the Wild.

As Hector searched the bookshelf, still more titles came simmered into being.

"Pretty amazing, isn't it?" Gaspar asked.

Hector nodded, but kept on searching. One glance revealed books on military history. Another found books about the ocean and the deep sea that Hector had been in love with as a boy and that his daughter was in love with. Another direction contained military thrillers, epic fantasies, and hard science fiction. He picked up a thin, black embossed volume of world history and flipped through the pages.

He paused at the table of contents. The words shimmered on the page like sunlight on the surface of a pond, each word coalescing when his eyes fell on it. Even stranger was that chapters and subchapters seemed like they were based on what Ramirez *wanted* to read and what he *wanted* to know. *History of the ancient world… Undiscovered Secrets… Politics of…* The words changed right before his eyes.

Hector turned to his grandfather, confusion and wonder on his face.

Gaspar smiled. "The Library of the Sun holds all the knowledge of everything that ever was and everything that ever will be. You only need to think of it, and a book will appear containing what you seek. This is the first Sphere of those that exemplified a virtue."

"And what virtue is that?"

"Prudence—the use of reason and diligence. The Library of the Sun is a place of philosophers, scientists, doctors, and all the righteous who sought knowledge. They sought to better understand the universe. Many would say that there's no more righteous goal than that.

"It's also the pursuit that is perverted the most. Many a politician and a salesman wound up in the City of Dis, started down that road by telling his patrons that he had all the answers or that they didn't really want to know the truth."

Hector nodded. He remembered looking down on the City of Dis in the Eighth Circle of Hell on the back of Geryon… It was only days ago, and yet it felt like another life to the soldier.

Ramirez turned and had begun to climb the stairs when Gaspar stopped him.

"Woah, Nieto. What do you think you'll find up there?" Gaspar's face was deadly serious.

Ramirez stood on the second step of the spiral staircase. Even though he was looking down on his abuelo, he felt like a boy again, wondering why he couldn't continue upward and keep looking.

"I... I don't know," Ramirez said honestly. "Can we go look?"

His grandfather's facade broke immediately to a smile. He waved dismissively. "Go on. Discovery is kind of the point here."

~

So, Ramirez wandered the library of the Sun, and at least for a while, forgot about his woes and reservations.

He walked through the aisles and picked at the shelves that had caught him initially, but then he looked through other corners, noticing that the shelves seemed to change and fill themselves as he walked.

But it wasn't just those! When Hector turned, wondering about the history of his family, he found volume after volume about the life of his ancestors. He picked up a volume about his great-great-grandfather Mateo, and saw the flickering table of contents organizing his life by decade. He had lived his early life in Chile before fleeing with his family to Mexico. But as Hector scanned the table of contents, he found the subchapters grew more intimate: *Greatest Joys. Thoughts on God. Marital Struggles. Disillusionment. Regrets.*

Hector hesitated reading further—hesitated even just scanning the table of contents. He had never met his great-great-grandfather Mateo, and it didn't feel right having access to such an intimate look at his life.

Gaspar eyed his grandson. The guide had been walking behind him on the stairs, perusing books but not picking any up to look at them.

"Even with lifetimes here in Heaven, there are many books that go unread."

Ramirez gently placed his great-great-grandfather's book back on the shelf. The soldier side-eyed Gaspar. "It seems like an invasion of privacy."

Gaspar chuckled. "It can be. But those who wind up here understand what they're looking for. Some might look to those private thoughts of another, not like a voyeur, but to seek to understand. A historian might look back at a portion of history, not just at the country, but at the people. The strife of the common people and that of the politicians can affect a greater whole. Remember Prudence. It isn't enough to seek knowledge and understanding. One must do it for the right reasons."

Ramirez nodded, his eyes falling back to the shelves again and the uncountable lifetimes of books that stretched out through the Library of the Sun.

Even the life story of his mother, grandfather Gaspar and grandmother Lucia appeared.

His mother's book, trimmed with red and pink. Her favorite colors. Hector had been about to reach for his mother's book, just to hold it, when he saw another green book sitting beside it. With the name of Diego. His father. The man he had never known.

Hector reached for it, only vaguely aware that his grandfather was staring at him tentatively. Ramirez pulled it out and held it gingerly with both hands, staring down at the plain letters of his father's book.

Ramirez turned the book over in his hands looking for details: Green. Simple dark orange font, same color line running around the outside. Nothing on the back—no writing, no design. He looked again to the other books on the shelf, to the empty space where his father's book belonged, and judged it was roughly the same size as the others. No longer, no shorter.

The man who left. The man Hector Ramirez would never know. Unless…

It would be an easy thing to open the book. To read it and get all the answers to all the questions that Ramirez had ever had about his father and about why he left.

His grandfather was still staring at him from a few steps below—Ramirez knew this—but he could turn away from the book. He'd said something about Prudence—about seeking knowledge for the right reasons.

But in that moment, holding the book and all the answers in his hands, his abuelo and his words were as distant as the stars. As distant as home.

And Hector Ramirez felt himself slowly drifting further away. He sat on the steps, continuing to stare at the cover and turn it over in his hands. His heart felt like it had dropped out of his chest.

He opened the book.

~

Diego Bustos
Born January 27th 1961. Died June 18th 2006.

Table of Contents

Early Life
  Parents
  Home in San Antonio

School
  Favorite Subjects
  Favorite Teachers
  Struggles with Bullies

Coming of Age
  First Love
  Odd Jobs
  Struggles with School

First Family
  Leaving
  Regrets

Second Family
  Second Chance
  Renewed Faith

Hector stared at the first page, mouth open, already regretting his decision and completely unable to stop, like his hands and eyes were moving on their own. He flipped through the first chapters, leafing through just fast enough that he couldn't read anything by the chapter titles.

He leafed through on autopilot until he came to the chapter titled, "First Family". Ramirez knew some things about his father, even some things about how his mother and father met. His mother told her boy long ago that whatever he wanted to know, she would tell him.

But Hector had never asked. Perhaps it was pride, or anger, or something else the young Hector didn't understand and the grown Hector had pushed aside.

He knew they met in grade school and were sweethearts for some months of high school. Past that he didn't want to know, or risk the book in his hands contradicting what his mother had told him.

As far as Hector cared, there was only one question. Why did his father leave?

Leaving

When Rosa told Diego that she was pregnant in the spring of 1962, Diego spiraled into depression. He felt he was too young. Not mature enough. Not ready. His mind was buried in turmoil.

Diego had been about to leave. About to break off their relationship. He couldn't stay with her. Worse—he couldn't face his parents.

Diego didn't go to school or speak to Rosa for two days.

When he finally worked up the courage to speak to her on the long walk home from school, it all came tumbling out. All his fears, all his worries. He didn't even get to the part about breaking up with Rosa, before she put a hand on his shoulder—stopping him.

Rosa said she was putting the baby up for adoption. She had already decided.

Diego was speechless.

Rosa told Diego that he didn't have to stay with her either.

Diego couldn't find the words. She left him, paralyzed with shock, on the edge of the grocery store parking lot.

They would pass each other by those last three months of school, smiling uneasily at one another, but never speaking. Diego's life continued on after that, without Rosa. And hers continued on as well.

Hector shook his head, sharing the same confusion. Obviously, his mother had kept Hector. He flipped forward to the chapter titled "Regrets".

Regrets

Diego would find out eight years later that Rosa had kept their baby. He wouldn't believe it until he saw her at the mall. She was pushing a baby stroller with a little boy in blue.

Diego froze—just like he had that fateful Spring day. When Rosa had left him, had told him she was giving up the baby for adoption. What she had really done was absolve him of his responsibilities.

He was frozen, heart dropped. Rosa saw him across the mall, waved at him, and then kept walking with her friend.

She had absolved Diego and forgotten about him.

Diego would see them only one more time before he left the state. He moved out to Texas.

He thought about Rosa and his son occasionally. Rarely when he meant to. Thoughts of them came unbidden, as bittersweet memories often did.

Sometimes he thought of finding Rosa again. Thought of asking for her back, of asking for forgiveness. But he never would.

No shit, Hector thought, book shaking in his hands. Quiet tears welled in his eyes. For a moment, Ramirez almost closed the book. What was the point in reading any more? His father wasn't around. No amount of reading would change that. So what was the point in continuing?

Begrudgingly, and without knowing why, Ramirez turned forward to the final chapter about his father's life. His "Second Family". This time, he quickly scanned the pages:

His father remarried almost ten years later. Three children. Swore to do everything right that time. Found his faith around the time his second child was born.

Ramirez flipped to the end.

Diego died of prostate cancer June 18th 2006.

He had a couple regrets. One of which was not knowing his son.

Currently resides in the Second Terrace of Purgatory.

"The bastard's in Purgatory," Hector said in disbelief.

For a flicker of a moment, his gaze met his grandfather's. But this time, Gaspar didn't chastise him—not for cursing or for being curious.

Ramirez stood on wobbly legs. He shut the book and stared at the cover. Squeezed his hands around the book, then hurled it over the railing and down to the floor.

The book fluttered open as it fell, then vanished before it hit the floor.

Ramirez looked around, confused. Then saw the book reappear on the shelf, right back beside his mother's book.

The soldier groaned and walked past his grandfather, down the golden stairs and back outside to the void-black surface.

Hector took one last contemptuous look up at the sprawling, gaudy M. C. Escher library of the Sun. Then he fell backward, phasing through the night-black surface, and reappearing on the surface of the sun.

~

Ramirez laid on the surface of the Sun, hands folded behind his head and looking up at the infinite void of space.

Trying not to think.

Sometime later—Ramirez had no idea just how long—Gaspar walked up and peered down at him. His abuelo's eyes were tired.

Hector rolled and pushed himself to his feet. "I didn't mean to worry you."

Gaspar just shook his head. "Doesn't matter. Did it help?"

Ramirez paced idly. He shook his head. "Doesn't matter."

"Of course it does."

"He left, Lito. He never came back."

Gaspar said, "But now you know. Does knowing why change anything?"

Hector searched himself. All the while he paced the surface of the Sun and his eyes looked everywhere except for at his grandfather.

He shrugged. "No. Guess I'm not going to wind up here, right?"

"Nieto…"

"Sorry," Hector said reflexively.

"Walk with me," Gaspar said, waving his grandson along. "Let's at least give you some direction."

Hector relented, and the pair walked slowly along the Sun.

"I can't speak for your father, Hector, but you have family that love you very much. Family that chooses to stay. And you know something? God loves you too, and he will always welcome you back. Always forgive you, if you look for it."

Hector nodded slightly, not to agree, but to acknowledge that he was listening.

"Have I ever told you about the metaphor of the train of life?"

Hector shook his head.

"Imagine life as a train. The trip is filled with stops and passengers. Some people ride the train with us for a long time, for many, many stops. Your mother was there the day you were born, and she'll be with you much longer still. Your abuela and I rode the train with you for a long time—as long as we could. Anna will ride with you for longer still.

"But not everyone rides the train with us for a long time. Childhood friends maybe only for a short while. People we know from church or the neighborhood might only be with us a few years. Acquaintances for even shorter. Some might only be on the train with us for a single stop. For a single afternoon.

"The really important thing, Hector, is to find those that want to be on the train with us. Those that help us when we need help, those that are there for us during the hard times and the joyous times. Those that make time for us, that choose to be with us.

"Choice, Nieto. Choice is the important thing."

They walked in silence, Gaspar letting his grandson digest his words, Hector turning them over in his head.

Choice.

Maybe that was why it hurt so much.

Hector finally said, "All my life I wondered why my father left. In a way, not knowing why was a blessing. That's why

Mom didn't tell me. Now I know that he chose to leave. He chose not to look for me."

"You chose not to look for him," Gaspar added quietly.

Ramirez nodded meekly.

"It's always about choice," Hector said.

"That's humanity's gift, Nieto. That's what sets us apart from everything else. Sure, we have urges and fears, but we can choose to ignore them and rise above them."

"Yeah…"

Hector stared at the night sky as they walked, even as a massive solar flare loomed on the horizon and the corner of his vision. He was looking past it, looking at the distant stars.

"Am I supposed to forgive him?" Ramirez turned to his grandfather, the question surprising both of them.

Gaspar shrugged. "That's your choice. But before you think more on it, remember two things: Remember that you can always change your mind. And that it's not necessarily that we owe people forgiveness but that we owe ourselves not to hold on to bitterness."

"I don't forgive him," Hector whispered. The words hung in the void. "He chose to leave. I'm choosing to deny him. To forget him."

His grandfather flinched ever so slightly at the words. "Apathy is a choice too."

"I… I think I'm ready to move on, Lito. Let's go to the next realm."

Gaspar nodded meekly, and both men looked to the stars before they left the surface of the Sun behind—perhaps forever.

~ ~ ~

Fifth Sphere:
Mars and the Warriors

The two men flew across pace in silence. The revelations of the prior Sphere weighed heavy on the soldier.

They passed by Mercury and Venus, and by Earth. Ramirez turned to watch the blue and white orb disappear behind them.

That was when he realized that flying was getting easier and less disorienting. Now it wasn't as necessary to keep his head fixed on the direction he was going.

Hector sighed. With each Sphere of Heaven, he was supposedly getting closer to God in the center, but he just felt further away.

He couldn't tell what he wanted more: To fly in silence so that he could try to zone out, or for his grandfather to talk to him and take his mind off of things.

Like so many other times, Hector Ramirez chose silence.

~

Mars came into view and the Red Planet didn't disappoint.

The planet was rust red as far as the eye could see. It wasn't until they were mid descent that Ramirez saw the terrain grow lively with dunes and pockmark craters. Closer still, and Hector finally saw buildings. These were a low-profile—barely a story tall—and all made of smooth, deep-black stone.

They landed on the dusty surface, just in front of one of the buildings. The stone was even smoother than it first appeared; there weren't any carvings or decorations adorning the surface. Even the lines of the stone blocks were difficult to see.

It was longer than Ramirez would admit before he realized what the structures reminded him of.

Bunkers. Hardened concrete bunkers.

From behind him, Gaspar said, "Mars is the Sphere of the warriors. Those who believed and were consistent in the virtue of Fortitude."

"It's a little on-the-nose, isn't it?" Ramirez asked, turning to the sprawling red desert. In the distance, he could just make out other low-profile black bunkers.

Gaspar shrugged. "Do you remember the surface of the Moon? Dusty, barren. Filled with buildings that stretched to the sky? Well, the Moon was for those that lacked Fortitude, those who were inconsistent. Mars recognizes those who were consistent in their faith. The buildings are low and humble. People spend their days making art and music below ground while warriors practice heavenly combat above. The surface is stained red with the blood of the faithful.

"It's not always literal warriors, but also those whose faith didn't waiver, no matter what happened in their lives.

"Listen," Gaspar said quietly.

Ramirez listened and heard music in the distance: The blaring of trumpets—intense and triumphant.

Gaspar said, "There is art and music here. And it is unlike anything seen in the earlier Spheres. It only gets better, Nieto. Do you feel anything yet?"

The soldier didn't recognize the song, nor could he deny that it was moving music. It was hard not to think back to military trumpets.

"Are you asking if I feel moved by the music or if I feel closer to God?"

His abuelo smiled widely. "They are one in the same."

Hector nodded. "I feel the music, but Lito…"

"What is it?"

"There are only faithful Christians here, right?"

Gaspar nodded.

"What about the people who fought bravely or gave their life for a comrade? What about sacrifice? What if they are on the wrong side? Or if they were born in the wrong place?"

"Nieto, Purgatory and Heaven are for believers. The righteous non-believers go to Limbo."

Ramirez shook his head. "The more I think about it, it just doesn't seem right."

His grandfather's voice was soft. "Many a fine soldier and good person have stayed in Purgatory or that First Circle of Hell. Those places aren't so bad, remember? They just aren't here."

"But if they're the same—if they're just as virtuous and good…"

"I told you earlier, Hector, don't presume to know His judgment."

"Virgil was right," Ramirez said.

Gaspar raised an eyebrow. "About what?"

Ramirez whispered, "That the Lord's mercy has limits."

Gaspar shook his head. "That's not the right way to think about it, Nieto. The Lord's mercy may have a requirement, but that's not the same. Don't forget that it's only by His grace anyone ascends.

Ramirez nodded, hands on his hips, but his mind was far away. He was looking out across the dunes of Mars and wondering just how many souls it took to stain the world red. Then thinking that there were so many more left behind.

Hector and his grandfather left the Sphere of Mars behind in all its barren red glory.

~ ~ ~

Sixth Sphere:
Jupiter and the Just

Again, the journey through space was quiet. This time Hector found himself wondering if that's what it would be like to actually fly through space aboard a spaceship. Would it be so quiet on the International Space Station, or was there background noise of the machines?

How long would it take astronauts to make the journey from planet to planet? Hector remembered faintly that the journey from Earth to Mars took almost a year.

"Lito, how fast are we going?"

Gaspar's face wrinkled in calculation. "Oh, a little faster than the speed of light, give or take. Why do you ask?"

"Just thinking about how long it would take for an astronaut to make this same journey." Ramirez glanced sideways at his abuelo. "If we can go so fast, why take any time to travel at all? Why not just teleport there. You know, like science fiction?"

Gaspar smirked. "So that we can have conversations like this! Just kidding. The real reason is *perspective*. If we teleported everywhere, all *willy-nilly*, then you would have no appreciation for just how vast the Universe is or how vast Heaven is. Or even how big the planets are!

"It's only with perspective that you can appreciate things. Without a journey, we can't appreciate a destination. Without a story, we can't appreciate the ending. If there were no suffering and no Hell, how could someone appreciate the good times and Heaven?"

Ramirez could tell that Gaspar wasn't through with that line of thinking—that his abuelo wanted a reply.

"I understand what you're saying. But what about the really bad times, Lito? What about the things that are so bad they destroy people?"

"Hector, I used to tell you that everything happens for a reason…"

"Yes, yes—'but it's only afterward that we can appreciate the reason'. I remember. *But…*"

"But that was the best I could explain it while I was alive. That's not the whole story. The other part of the problem is Free Will. You mustn't think of those horrible things as part of God's plan. It's more like people mucking it up. Remember the Virtues, Hector. There are people who exemplify the Heavenly Virtues, and people who give in to Sins."

"What about the good times, then?" Ramirez asked. "Does God claim credit for those?"

Gaspar narrowed his eyes at his grandson. "A little more credit than He claims for the bad things. Let me ask you this, Nieto. When Anna was little, how much credit did you claim for her behavior? Surely you praised her when she listened and scolded her when she didn't. But did you claim credit for every good thing and every bad thing? Of course not. No matter how well you taught her, there were times she didn't listen and times she grew beyond her years."

Hector dwelled on this a moment, but thinking of his daughter and his wife were not helping him sort his thoughts. "Is that where the metaphor of God as the Heavenly Father comes from?"

Gaspar nodded. "More or less. We may not always listen, but God is guiding us toward a better path."

"Why not give us better guide rails, then? Some suffering I can understand… but war, rape, genocide?"

Gaspar shook his head. "Free Will is the most powerful force the Universe has ever seen. Just look at what humankind has been able to accomplish in such a relatively short time! But it's a tool like anything else. And in the wrong hands, Free Will can be a weapon.

"And think of this, Hector, that Free Will is constrained enough already. People are only capable of so much. We're not omniscient like the Lord or even very strong like some of the lesser deities that walked the Earth. Our bodies are limited by our genes, and our minds are limited by our environment. Even our behavior is limited by our laws and our culture.

"And lastly I must remind you: Don't presume to know the Lord."

Hector turned his eyes forward, dejected. As if on cue, the swirling Sphere of Jupiter appeared in the distance.

~

The largest planet in the solar system—the Sixth Sphere of Heaven—swirled enormous in the sky. The surface was covered in clouds like Venus, but Jupiter's clouds swirled around furiously. This storm churned around the planet in bands of color—yellows and blues, and reds and browns. As they descended, Hector kept thinking that they would pass through the clouds at any second, but the planet was so large that the clouds played tricks on his eyes.

For a moment, it felt like he was going back to the Sun again. *That* was how large Jupiter felt. Even though the soldier knew that the Sun was many times bigger, Jupiter was so large that it might as well have been the same to him.

When he and his grandfather finally slipped into the clouds, they too took forever to pass.

When they slipped through the clouds completely, the ground was already beneath them. Hector looked around in disbelief—on Earth and on Venus, the clouds hung miles above the surface. On Jupiter, the clouds were more like fog, and seemed to swirl only a few feet above his head.

The ground was paved in purple and gold as far as Ramirez could see. Nearby was a thin purple tower, no more than three stories tall. Clouds spewed from the top the same color as the clouds that swirled above. Similar towers dotted the horizon, each with thin wisps of clouds rising

"What is that, Lito?" Hector asked.

That is a monument and throne for one of the just rulers.

Ramirez walked over to the tower hesitantly. There was a small open doorway through which he peered. Inside was a small living quarters. Bed, table, chairs adorned the room, while a tall golden throne overlooked it. Sitting on the throne was a dark-skinned man with a long beard, wearing white robes, and sitting very still—he didn't even appear to be breathing.

Moments later, two ghostly men walked through another opening on the opposite side of the room. They might've been speaking Latin or Greek—though Hector could only guess at the real answer. Though he couldn't understand them, from their gestures the two men appeared to be friends.

One of them was the same bearded man that stared placidly from atop the throne.

"I don't understand," Ramirez mumbled.

Gaspar put a hand on his shoulder. "Jupiter is the Sphere for just rulers. For those who exemplified the virtue of Justice. Here, the entire world is paved in the colors of gold and royalty. The sky above is filled with clouds so that the rulers of the past only need to concern themselves with those things nearby instead of so many things like they did when they were alive. It is a respite for them.

"It is one thing to live justly and to believe rightly, but it is another to govern others in a just manner. It's as true a measure of a person as being a parent is the true measure of a mother and a father.

"Don't you see the difference between Mercury and here?"

Ramirez nodded slowly. "I guess so."

"What's the matter?"

The soldier stared across the landscape. "It just feels a lot different from what I expected. There's so many different ideas about Heaven… But I guess Hell and Purgatory were the same way. None of it was what I expected."

"Don't forget, Nieto, that all of this, every Sphere of Heaven is with the Lord. Each Sphere dwells within Him and all feel His light…

"Don't you feel it, Hector?"

For a moment, Hector wasn't sure what to say. But when he glanced to his abuelo, he knew that the old man deserved nothing but the truth.

Ramirez shook his head. "I don't feel anything. I barely felt the clouds when we flew through them. What does that mean?"

Gaspar shook his head quickly. "Nothing, Hector. You're still conflicted, that's all."

The soldier nodded wearily. He was conflicted. Flying through Heaven had almost had the opposite effect on his faith. He was more conflicted now than he'd ever been.

Each Sphere reminded him less and less of home. Each felt more and more removed from the humanity that Ramirez knew. If anything, each successive Sphere felt more and more like the strange demiplanes of creatures from his past in Omega squad.

~ ~ ~

Seventh Sphere: Saturn and the Contemplatives

Quiet hung over the two men as they flew through the void of space.

"I'm sorry," Ramirez finally said.

Gaspar looked over, wearing a look of concern. "For what, Nieto?"

"This probably isn't going the way you expected. Bringing me up to Heaven, I mean. Probably expected me to sing during these journeys between Spheres," he added sheepishly.

Gaspar smirked and shook his head. "I admit, this hasn't gone the way I thought it would go. But I should've known better. When you were growing up, you were always questioning things. You used to drive me loco sometimes. 'But Lito' this, 'but Lito' that. Your abuela used to call me 'But Lito' when I was in a bad mood—snapped me right out of it."

Hector chuckled and felt his chest relax, if only slightly.

"Truly Nieto, I should've known better. I should've known this would be hard for you. Or at the very least, that it wouldn't be easy. Some people, all they have to do is see it. All they have to do is see Heaven or Hell, and they're convinced. Of course, there are others that never question their faith to begin with, and that's its own bag.

"But you… You need to feel that it's right. You need to be one hundred percent certain that it's right. Don't you?"

"I guess so."

"And that's the problem, I think. You'll never get to one hundred percent—that's why it's called faith. Doubt occupies that last little bit, that uncertainty. Faith might not assuage your doubt, but it papers over it like a good paint job."

"Lito… Virgil told me that there were others like me that had journeyed through Hell, through Purgatory, and through Heaven. Did you know any of them?"

Gaspar shook his head. "Virgil leads most everyone through the lower planes, and someone close to them leads them through Heaven. Most anyone who's anyone knows about Dante Alighieri's journey; I've only heard rumors about the others."

"Does everyone make it? Through Hell and all the way through Heaven, I mean?"

His grandfather thought on this as they flew through space. Finally, he said, "Some people don't. Some get stuck in Purgatory. Most people make it through the entire journey. But if you want to know if everyone believes at the end of the journey? …Well, not everyone has a change of heart by the end."

Ramirez was shocked. It was one thing for him to have doubts, but for others to make the same journey as him…

It meant that he wasn't alone in his crisis.

"So, what happens when someone gets all the way to the end and they still don't believe?" Hector asked. "Does God just let them go?"

Gaspar nodded. "It's their choice, Nieto. Simple as that. And if they eventually change their mind, God will accept them into Heaven. That's what I meant before about His mercy.

"Look," Gaspar said, pointing off in the distance. "We're nearly there."

~

Saturn rose from the black.

Compared to the turbulence of Jupiter, Saturn looked like a photograph. A yellow-orange sphere, surrounded by a plate of silver rings—

At least that's how it looked from far away.

As they flew closer and closer to the rings, Hector felt like his eyes were playing tricks on him. The area of the rings nearby faded from view—completely disappeared—while he could still see the outline and color of the rings at the edges of the horizon.

"Lito… How is that possible?" Hector asked, pointing out the illusion.

"The rings are made up mostly of very small stones. Up close, they're hard to see. But far away, you can see the culmination of billions and trillions of particles."

"I guess that makes sense," the soldier replied tentatively.

Gaspar shrugged. "Hey, I'm no scientist. I'm just giving you the tour."

Gaspar led Hector past the things and down toward the clouds. Ramirez looked up to see one last glimpse of the rings, and saw them from directly between the planet and the rings.

To him, they appeared like ultra-thin rings wrapping around the planet, or like the backbone of night stretching across the heavens.

Then they disappeared as the two men dipped below the orange clouds.

~

Ramirez didn't speak as they descended through the clouds. The clouds of Saturn were still and smelled of salt. For the first time, he felt warmth in the clouds.

When they finally broke through to the surface, Ramirez found a world of endless white sand. Rather than dunes, the sand was hard packed beneath his boots, like that of a shoreline. And in the distance, at the farthest edge of the horizon, he could see shimmering water. There was nothing else save for barren sand.

"Wow," Hector whispered. "Where are all the buildings? Where are all the people?"

"Well, there's not as many here as there are on Venus, that's for sure. There's people here, it's just that—of all the virtues, Temperance is one of the hardest to practice because it requires not just dedication to a single thing or refraining from a single act. It requires total dedication.

"If you actually stayed a while and talked to some of the souls here, you'd find there's not a lot different from them and the saints in the next Sphere."

Ramirez turned around in a complete circle, scanning the horizon. "So, what.. They just walk around all day, thinking deep thoughts?"

Gaspar shrugged.

"Come on, Lito. You're messing with me."

Gaspar held up his hands in mock defense. "Hey, when you're this close to the Lord, that's all you need. No—In all seriousness, Nieto, people that made it this far, dedicated so much of their waking life to the Lord, that it's hard to relate. Lots of philosophers and monks and nuns.

"Remember too, that all Spheres exist in the heart of the Lord. Furthermore, all Spheres can talk with one another. If for some reason, family found themselves on another Sphere, it's not like they're closed off from one another. It's possible to visit, you know."

Ramirez tried to think of what it would be like to wander the endless beach and he was drawn back to his time in Hell— to his time walking across the endless beach of the Seventh Circle of Hell, where the violent burned for eternity in the lake of fire.

"Lito, what do they say about fate? About Determinism— I think that's the word."

"I imagine most of it is chalked up to Free Will. Why do you ask?"

Ramirez turned to his grandfather. "To wind up on this Sphere or on Jupiter with the just rulers, I imagine you have to be pretty lucky. I mean, you have to work hard and dedicate your life... But you also have to be lucky. I never had a chance to be a monk. I never had a chance to be a king."

"I think you misunderstood me, Hector. It's not only kings or queens or mayors that make it to Jupiter. There are managers, heads of family, parents, even good friends. Here on Saturn, it's not just philosophers and monks. Anyone that exemplifies the Virtues can wind up here."

"But what about people that have harder lives than others? You have to admit that not everyone has the same life."

Gaspar nodded. "That's why all you need to do is believe in the Lord and try to live a decent life."

"And all the Spheres exist within the Lord…" Hector trailed off, nodding slightly. He *got it*, or at least thought he did.

He just couldn't help but think of all the damned people he had seen in Hell. Or of all the people he had seen in Purgatory, spending lifetimes struggling to make it to the next Terrace or having given up altogether and resigned themselves to an afterlife on the mountain.

"Still not convinced?" Gaspar asked with a hint of playfulness on his face. "That's okay, because we're still not done. The closer we get to the center, the more you'll understand."

Hector merely nodded.

For all their talk of Free Will, Ramirez felt that he had very little of it.

He had gone through Hell, climbed Purgatory, and now he was flying across Heaven—all at the whim of others.

Hector kept his mind focused on the mission, as he had so many other times. He had to see the mission through—one last mission. He had to get home to Tracey and Anna. And he imagined that what happened then would be out of his hands as well.

~ ~ ~

Eighth Sphere:
The Fixed Stars and
the Saints

They left Saturn behind. The clouds and the rings receded until they reminded Hector of photographs he'd seen as a boy. The beauty of seeing the rings above him like a backbone of the sky, the feeling of walking across the endless beach… all of it faded, until it was nothing more than a smudge in the sky.

Ramirez looked behind him and watched even the sun fading until it was a speck, and then further until it was just another star in the sky.

Somehow, Hector knew they had left the solar system behind, that they had flown immensely farther and faster than during any of their previous trips.

Gaspar and Hector slowed to a stop. And for the first time, the soldier felt something faint—like a warm breeze across his skin or sun on his face. *It was warmth*, but it almost felt like a trick or a hallucination. If it wasn't for the stillness of space and absence of feeling, Ramirez doubted he would have noticed it at all.

"Is... Is this the next Sphere?"

"Yes," Gaspar said, slowing down until they hung in the empty void of space.

"I think I feel what you were talking about," Hector whispered, as if speaking too loud might break the illusion.

His grandfather nodded. "That's the Light."

But more than the Light, Hector felt a sense of vastness—of emptiness.

He had seen planets packed full of people, but as they ascended through the Spheres, each planet seemed a little more empty than the last. And now, they were hanging in empty space.

"Lito, *where* are we?"

"This is the Sphere of the saints, Nieto. The realm of the Fixed Stars."

"Are each of the stars saints?"

"Oh no. Only some. Most are just other stars."

As Ramirez looked across the stars, he could feel some of the saints utter their names: James, Peter, and John. Each spoke in a whisper, and even though they were far away and spoke little, Ramirez saw flashes of their lives.

"Why are they so *distant*?" Ramirez finally asked. They felt far away in both body and mind.

"Do you remember the mountain of Ostia?" Gaspar asked, to which Hector nodded. "The last Terrace of Purgatory was about forsaking Earthly connections. So very few pass through those gates and it is the same here. So very few give themselves so wholly and completely to God as the saints do. They are very near angels in that sense—arbiters of the Lord.

"That is why they feel so far away, because they are very different from you or I. In that respect, Nieto, you do have to be a special person to be counted here. Anyone can be accepted into Heaven, but I don't think that everyone can become a saint."

Ramirez swept his gaze across the stars. Though he couldn't see the planets any longer, he knew without a doubt which star was the Sun. That tiny little speck, indistinguishable from all the other stars in the sky.

For a moment, Hector was swept up in the vastness. For a moment, he forgot about going home, and about confronting Tracey about her infidelity and about their marriage. He forgot about getting home to his daughter.

All those things seemed lost in the bigger picture. He couldn't see Earth anymore. How could he possibly keep all those other things in perspective?

His time in Omega Squad seemed small in comparison. He'd seen things people wouldn't believe—not in their wildest dreams and most horrific nightmares. Strange demiplanes and supernatural beings, even some that rivaled angels and demons. But all of them were impossibly small from so far away.

Ramirez said idly, "So few can see the world like this, is that it? So few can detach themselves so much from the world."

"Few indeed," Gaspar replied. "On Earth, we're so preoccupied with the little things. School, work, family. We forget just how big the world really is. A person can only see the bigger picture by detaching themselves from the smaller ones."

"What about God then? Does that mean he's detached?"

Gaspar shook his head. "No, Nieto. God is love. Just because people cannot hold those two opposing views of the world doesn't mean that He can't.

"How many people do you love?" Gaspard asked.

Ramirez counted on his fingers. "Anna… Tracey… You, Mama Lucia. My mother…"

"It's not possible to love more. Not really. The saints are the only people that come close to both loving God and their fellow people. But that's not it all either. It's not enough to love your fellow people, because you do not truly *know them*."

Hector shook his head. "I don't understand, Lito."

"Now that you know your father, do you love him? Did you ever love him?"

Hector's stomach dropped and his mouth hung open. It felt like he'd been punched in the gut and scolded as a child again. He was supposed to love his father, right? Even the Bible said so.

He had never loved his father. Not when he was an angry boy, and not now that he was a bitter man. Hector didn't want to forgive the man, and Hector didn't think he would ever love his father.

Ramirez just shook his head. He couldn't say the words out loud or even meet his grandfather's eyes.

"That's God, Nieto. God loves your father. He recounted and asked for forgiveness, and God loves him. The Lord can do the hard things. Only God can raise us up from Hell."

"Infinite mercy," Ramirez whispered quietly. *For those that believed.*

And one soldier floating in the abyss of space, so close to God, couldn't bring himself to accept it.

~ ~ ~

Ninth Sphere: The First Moved and the Angels

Ramirez didn't think that it was possible to feel further away from home, but then he had been wrong many times throughout his journey. At first, he thought Gaspar was merely leading him deeper into space, but then the stars began to disappear.

The void of night sky became awash in swirls of color. Greens, yellows, and reds ebbed and flowed like oil dripped onto water, like great tides churning in the cosmos.

Hector's eyes opened wide. He'd seen a view like this before when he was in school. The great swirls of color were whole galaxies' worth of stars and nebulas of gas that hadn't yet coalesced into galaxies. He felt like a giant standing amidst the universe—not seeing individual stars and planets, but billions of them churning and boiling together.

Dots of light flashed in one of the gas clouds, like diamonds glittering. "Lito, what are those?"

"Those are stars being born, Hector," his grandfather whispered. Gaspar watched the scene intently too.

Ramirez turned. All around him were enormous swirls of colors. The twinkle of stars being born, and great flashes as they went supernova and died.

Hector wasn't sure how long he watched the Sphere unfold around him, only that neither of them spoke again for a long time.

Not until it dawned on him just how long was passing. "Lito, we're not looking at time the same way either, are we?"

"No, we're not. Many thousands of years are passing with each blink." Gaspar turned to his grandson. "Don't worry, you can always go back. It's not like Earth is gone." He smiled sheepishly.

Something soared above them, leaving a sweeping, fading wake behind it. At first, Hector thought it was a comet because of the tail, but there was no way a comet could be so big—not on the size of galaxies.

All Ramirez had to do was point, and Gaspar knew his question.

"That's an angel."

Hector stared at it, but couldn't see the shape of the angel itself. it seemed shrouded, or warped... little more than a blur. All he could make out was the enormous wake—if a word could do the scale of it justice. It dragged whole nebulas and galaxies along with it.

Gaspar said, "Do you remember how you could barely see the saints? Well, the angels look the way they do because they are even more different from us. They're more like forces of nature than people."

Hector listened, and as his grandfather spoke, he again felt warmth on his face like he had in the Sphere of the Saints. Only this time, it was more. It felt close enough that he could reach out and grasp the sun.

In that moment, Ramirez saw dozens—hundreds—of angels sweeping across the cosmos. All circling a single incomprehensible ball of light.

That light was God. And the angels swept outward from it.

They're more like forces of nature than people. Gaspar's voice echoed in his head.

"There's no Free Will here, is there?" Ramirez asked.

"Free Will is the great separator between humans and angels," Gaspar replied plainly.

Ramirez thought back to the Sphere of Fixed stars and the Saints, and then Saturn and the Contemplatives before that. There was something building in these last few Spheres of Heaven—the detachment from Earthly concerns and the lack of Free Will. The planets growing more and more barren...

It felt like being closer to God necessitated being detached from the world. To be closer to God, one had to give up more and more of their Free Will—

Only those that believe can get into Heaven.

"What's the matter, Nieto?" Gaspar asked, quietly.

Hector turned and saw his grandfather floating beside him. And Hector smiled at the deep set wrinkles in his abuelo's face, the rolled-up sleeves of his flannel shirt. It was such a strange thing to see the man who meant so much to him, who had helped him through so much, against the backdrop of the universe.

Gaspar's face turned sullen, the faint frown taking eons to form. "You still don't feel the Light?"

And he read Hector's face plainly.

"Oh God, I've failed you," Gaspar whispered. "I've failed you."

"No, no, Lito," Ramirez said. He floated over and embraced his abuelo. "I am a man. Not an angel or a saint. It's my choice. *It's my choice*," Hector said again to himself.

Hector held his grandfather tightly, just like he had when he was a boy. Like all those countless times Hector had come crying to him as a young boy and as a young man. Now it was the soldier's turn to do the same.

"Of all the things I've seen," Hector said. "I'm glad I got to see you and Mama Lucia again. That would've been enough to go through Hell and back again."

Eternity passed before Gaspar's breathing slowed. Longer still until Hector and he let go of each other.

Gaspar wiped his eyes and nodded. Then he took his grandson to meet the Lord.

~ ~ ~

Empyrean

As Ramirez and Gaspar flew, the Universe grew small around them. The enormous swathes of color, billowing nebulas and churning galaxies shrunk until they were nothing more than candle smoke.

They flew past the billowing contrails of angels and toward the single ball of light—the light of the Lord. And it grew large and blinding as if they were flying into the heart of the Sun.

Only that in the center of the sun, Ramirez had been able to see. Here the world was blinding white and gold.

"Where are we, Lito?"

"In the center of Heaven. We are with Him and within Him."

The light blazed all around, except for beneath Ramirez. There, the soldier saw a shimmering surface—a translucent pond, only six feet across. Even though the light around him was blinding, Hector could just see through the water's surface. Beyond lay the Universe—all the galaxies and nebulas and stars that he had just flown through; all of them condensed and swirling like the cloudy waters of a pond.

It reminded Hector of standing on the surface of the Sun again. In a way, that had been a glimpse of God.

The soldier turned back to the blinding sky, and again felt warmth. This time, the sensation seemed to seep through his skin, to fill him. To ease his weariness.

It felt as if he were hugging his grandfather again. It was then that he believed his grandfather's words. All the Universe, all the Spheres of Heaven dwelled inside God. They all felt His Light.

Tears streamed down Ramirez's face because of the beauty of His Light. Because Ramirez had gone so long without feeling it.

And tears because even after seeing the Light of the Lord, Hector Ramirez did not believe.

Because he hoped that seeing the face of God would be enough to change his mind. That the Light would reveal something more to him. But there was no answer to his questions, no great revelation.

Instead, Hector found that his revelations had already been found...

Virgil had once said to him that there are no perfect persons in Heaven. That all people had their shortcomings. But there are equally good persons in the Circle of Limbo, for no other reasons other than their birthrights.

Rather than lifting all souls from Hell, God required that people believe in Him.

Virgil had also said that if God's mercy had limits, that He was no different from any of the other gods that came before or will come to pass.

A being of infinite mercy shall not require anything of me, Virgil had said.

And God was silent.

The blinding light that surrounded Hector dimmed slightly—just enough for Hector to see his grandfather. Gaspar was staring at him with a pleading look on his face.

"I… I don't believe," Ramirez said. "Not now. Maybe one day, but not now. That's my choice, Lito. I have to get home. I have to get back to Tracey and Anna. *I'm choosing to go home.*"

Years of love hung between them, mirrored by the two men.

Gaspar smiled painfully. "I love you, Hector."

"I love you, Lito."

The light vanished and Hector fell. The Universe grew around him again—swirls of smoke blossoming until they filled his vision and continued until they became unfathomable clouds and galaxies again. Then even those vanished, and the sky was once again black and filled with stars.

~ ~ ~

Free Will

When Hector finally came to, he was walking down the street. Still wearing his fatigues and boots, as he always had been.

He glanced around, seeing the grid-patterned streets of suburbia for the first time... Well, for the first time in months, though it felt like years. Crisp square yards lined the sidewalk. Blue cloudless sky above.

Finch street sign stood just ahead.

His street.

It felt like a dream. No one ever remembers how dreams start.

Virgil Maro's words echoed in his head: *"The River of Forgetfulness is not for the pain. It is so you do not remember the Hollows. So you do not remember the way out of Hell.*

"You will not know how far you have walked or how much time has passed, but one day you will be through the Hollows. You will find yourself standing in a field with the sun on your face, wondering how you could have possibly made it through all that you have suffered, all that you have seen and felt and lived.

"But you will have made it, all the same."

Ramirez hadn't remembered the journey out of Hell or the fall from Heaven. But as he felt the warm sun on his face and tears on his cheek, Ramirez knew he was home.

Virgil had been right—about everything except standing in a field.

Ramirez's walk turned into a jog as he rounded the corner to Finch Street and then jogged three houses down to his house.

And at the end of the driveway, Hector Ramirez froze. He looked at his green split foyer house, taking in the sight of it, and realized that Tracey's car was in the driveway.

She was inside.

Hector's heart was pounding, his throat dry, his hands clammy.

More than all the Spheres of Heaven, he had longed to get home and run inside. More than all the Terraces of Purgatory, he had prepared himself for confronting Tracey. And more than all the Circles of Hell, he was terrified of what was about to happen.

Tracey walked up to the window, and for a moment, her eyes mirrored his own.

Then she ran out the door, and clung to the porch railing.

"Hector…?" she said, so quietly that Ramirez could barely hear her.

She was wearing a plain yellow dress. Even wide-eyed and in shock, she was beautiful—the most beautiful thing Hector had ever seen.

She walked across the driveway, hands to her mouth in shock. "Oh, Hector." And she held out her arms.

Hector and Tracey embraced, holding each other tight. The lavender smell of her hair was all he could think about.

God, he was home.

And home wasn't really his anymore.

And Hector held his wife, all the same.

When Tracey finally pulled away, she still held his arms. Quiet tears streamed down her face.

"They wouldn't tell me what happened," she whispered. "They said you were missing. God, they wouldn't tell me. Not about you or Atticus or…"

"I'm here," Hector said reflexively, his heart sinking at the mention of Atticus.

He looked to the house, realization slowly dawning on him of the conversation they were about to have, all the things he had to tell her—that Hector knew, and that Atticus was dead…

"Come on," Tracey said, tugging his arm. "Let's go inside."

Hector walked beside her, arm in arm, up to the house.

~

Tracey led him through the front door, past the potted plants on the mantle and her romance book on the couch. He followed her in a haze and sat at the dining room table, boots still on.

"I'll put on a pot of coffee," Tracey said, walking over to the counters.

Ramirez turned and looked across the living room for Anna, but remembered that it was midday. She was at school. Of course she was.

So he waited for Tracey to put on coffee, alternating between watching her and staring at the refrigerator.

Being home still felt like a dream. Still felt like the Hollows.

Tracey came over and sat to his right, her hands clasped nervously on the table. "Are you okay?"

Hector couldn't bring himself to look at her as he recounted pieces of what happened. "It was bad, Trace. I... I don't remember how I got home. We lost everybody... Everybody."

The words hung between them like ghosts. Ramirez wasn't sure what else to say. He just let the silence fill in the rest.

Slowly, Tracey's eyes grew wider and wider, first in suspicion, then in shock, and finally, in disbelief.

"How?" She stuttered. "Oh, God..." Tracey's eyes watered.

Ramirez's heart was in his throat.

"It doesn't matter," Tracey whispered, eyes clamped shut. "It doesn't matter."

"Tracey..."

She looked up at Hector, eyes pleading. Like they might've been full of hope or terror. Hope that he didn't know. Or terror that he did.

Hector offered his hands on the table and Tracey took them. The fear in her eyes turned to sadness, as if she already knew the answer.

"It's okay, Trace. I know about you and Atticus. I found out on the mission."

As the words sank in, finding their places with the other ghosts between them, Ramirez didn't pull away, and neither did Tracey.

It was a long time between quivering breaths before anyone spoke.

Tracey's voice was barely a whisper. "I'm so, so sorry." She said it three times before her face wrinkled in anguish.

"It's okay, Trace," Hector said slowly, staring mostly at his wife's hands in his. "I had time to come to terms with it. I should've seen that something was wrong. *I should've asked.* God, I should've asked."

"I should've talked to you," she said.

"I wasn't here. When I was home, I wasn't here—not like I should've been. But I'm here now. And, I just want to say that I'm sorry to have to tell you like this—to tell you all this.

"I love you, and Atticus was my best friend, but it happened and it can't go back to the way it was. I don't think—I don't know."

Tracey squeezed his hands, then pulled away. She leaned back in the chair. Hands clutched to her face, chest heaving.

Hector wanted to hold her, but he didn't. He felt frozen again.

Tracey's chest finally slowed, and she pulled her hands away from her face, makeup running.

Ramirez met her eyes. "Where do we go from here, Trace? Can we… Can we work on things?"

"I don't know, Hector." Tracey glanced away from him. "Seeing you after all this… I don't know. I was going to ask you…" She couldn't finish the sentence.

"I know," Hector whispered. "Atticus told me."

It didn't really matter how Ramirez had found out—Atticus telling him or learning it in Purgatory.

"It's okay, Trace. I had some time," Hector said again. "I just want you to know that you and Anna mean the world to me, and that I'll be there for you, and for our daughter. But it's your choice, Trace. It's your choice."

Tracey sighed, and the quiver in her breathing lessened.

When the moment had long passed and some of the ghosts between them had faded, Tracey stared at him with bloodshot eyes.

"What happened out there?"

Too much, Hector thought. Tracey would think he was nuts. How could he even begin to tell her?

And so Hector went back to his old lines. "I don't know how much I can tell you. But it doesn't matter. What happened, happened.

"...Can I stay here a few days, Trace?"

She nodded. "Of course. I... God, I haven't told Anna anything yet."

Without hesitation, Hector replied, "We can tell her together."

~

Ramirez walked outside and sat on the front steps of the porch. For a moment, it felt like he was back in the Hollows, waiting for Anna's bus. He'd been on the porch the last half an hour, thinking about the events culminating in this moment.

Hector Ramirez had gone to Hell because he was told to, and then to Purgatory and Heaven for the same reason. He had chosen to come home, despite how hard the journey had been, and despite how nothing would ever be the same.

Ramirez's sin was that he didn't act. He didn't use his Free Will. He didn't tell his wife his true feelings back when it mattered, that he knew they were drifting apart.

Free Will was nothing unless it was used.

Hector had stood in Empyrean, in the heart of God, and chosen to come home. Chosen not to believe—despite all that he had seen and lived.

But then, belief was supposed to be done without evidence. There it was again: *Choice*.

Tracey chose to leave him, and Hector was going to let her go.

Just like Hector chose to leave God, and the Lord let him go.

And both parents would be there for Anna.

Ramirez hoped the warmth of the sun meant he was doing the right thing.

A few minutes later, Anna's bus pulled up to the curb. Anna stepped out. She stopped on the curb, and for a moment, it felt like time had frozen.

Anna smiled and ran up to hug her father, and he stooped down to meet her. The pair wrapped their arms around each other.

In that moment, Hector had faith that everything would turn out alright.

END OF TRILOGY

Thank you for Reading

If you enjoyed this story, I would greatly appreciate a short review on Amazon or your favorite book website. Reviews are crucial for any author, and even just a line or two can make a huge difference.

Looking for more Strange Places?

You might like **Tales from Another World**. It's a ongoing collection of Fantasy short stories, all set in the same world.

Live the lives of sorcerers, druids, barbarians, strange creatures, gods, ghosts, and commoners caught in between.

If you're in the mood for an ongoing serial, check out **A Battleaxe and a Metal Arm**. I plan on including lots of strange, awe-inspiring and eerie locations in each one. It's got a little more action than some of the other fantasy stories, but no less strangeness.

A sorceress with a metal arm and a barbarian with a battle-axe stuck in an endless, changing dungeon. *Come for the action. Stay for the mystery.*

On writing
Unto Heaven

Sometimes things have strange beginnings.

Who knew that a young writer's idea of special forces soldiers journeying into Hell would turn into a reimagining of Dante's Divine Comedy—eventually shucking the action to critique the idea of Free Will in Christianity?

I didn't.

The more I thought about why Lieutenant Ramirez lost his faith, the more I turned it over in my head, the more I realized I had to explore it. I had to write it.

From there it became a back and forth about whether he would find his faith again—will he or won't he?

Now, traditional Christian literature (at least most everything I can find) always goes toward finding faith again. But the more I wrote and the further Ramirez journeyed, the more I realized it wasn't about finding his faith, it was about getting home to Tracey and Anna. It had turned into finding out what was truly important to Ramirez, and his family was more important. There was just one problem:

As much as Ramirez wanted to go back to Tracey and Anna—that he chose to go back—Tracey could choose to leave. Free Will works both ways.

Ultimately, there's always a chance that Ramirez might find his faith again, just like his father, Diego did. I wanted to leave that open to interpretation. But ultimately, that is where the story ended, with the parallel of Ramirez leaving God, and Tracey leaving her husband.

Not that husbands are equivalent to God or anything—don't read too much into it. I just liked the parallel.

Anyway, thanks for coming along for the journey.

~ Sam

Further Reading

If you're interested in reading the original Dante's *Inferno* (or the entire *Divine Comedy*) then you're in luck, because you can find it in the classics for section for free. It's quite a bit different than the story you just read, but it's great in its own right (a classic for a reason). If you find the poetry hard to parse, then you can look for abridged versions or even summaries to get you through it.

Connect with the Author

If you want to stay up to date on the latest about Samuel's publishing news and blog, check out his website and consider signing up for his monthly newsletter.

www.SamuelFlemingBooks.com

Samuel can also be found on Reddit, Goodreads and Facebook.

Samuel Fleming is a Science Fiction and Fantasy author.

He grew up in Maryland, spending most of his time swimming and writing. Swimming gave him a lot of time to daydream, so the two hobbies complemented each other well. Idle day dreams turned into stories, some of which stuck with him for years. These days he swims a little less and writes a lot more.

He loves a good story no matter the medium: Books, TV, video games, comics, tabletop RPG's, or podcasts—most of which he attempts to share with his wife and three kids, and occasionally on his blog.

CPSIA information can be obtained
at www.ICGtesting.com
Printed in the USA
LVHW012102240322
714286LV00005B/598